SKY HIGH

by GERMANO ZULLO / *illustrated by* ALBERTINE

CHRONICLE BOOKS
SAN FRANCISCO

First published in the United States in 2012 by Chronicle Books LLC.
Originally published under the title *Les Gratte-Ciel* in 2011 by Editions La Joie de lire SA., 5 chemin Neuf, -1207
Genève - Switzerland.

Library of Congress Cataloging-in-Publication Data available.

ISBN: 978-1-4521-1392-0

Manufactured in China.

10 9 8 7 6 5 4 3

Chronicle Books LLC
680 Second Street
San Francisco, CA 94107

www.chroniclebooks.com

Agenor-Agobar Poirier des Chapelles' house

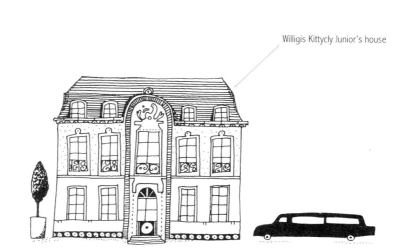

Willigis Kittycly Junior's house

Solid
gold door

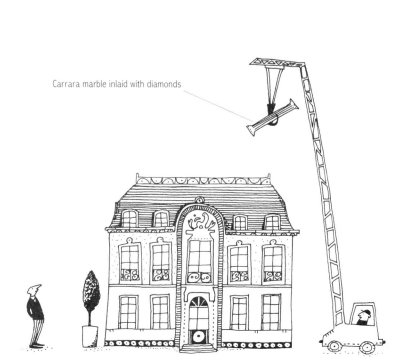

Carrara marble inlaid with diamonds

Construction ladder

Arthur J. Sciacallo,
the highest paid
architect in the world

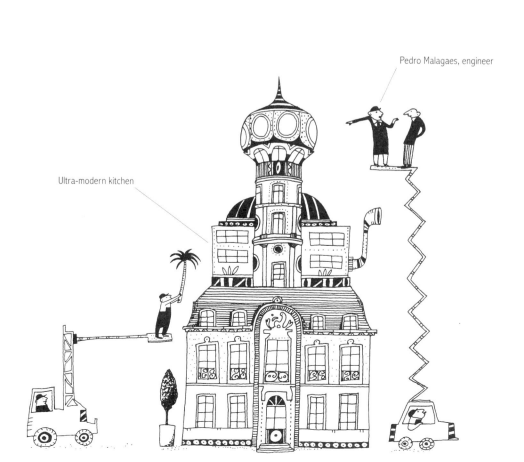

Pedro Malagaes, engineer

Ultra-modern kitchen

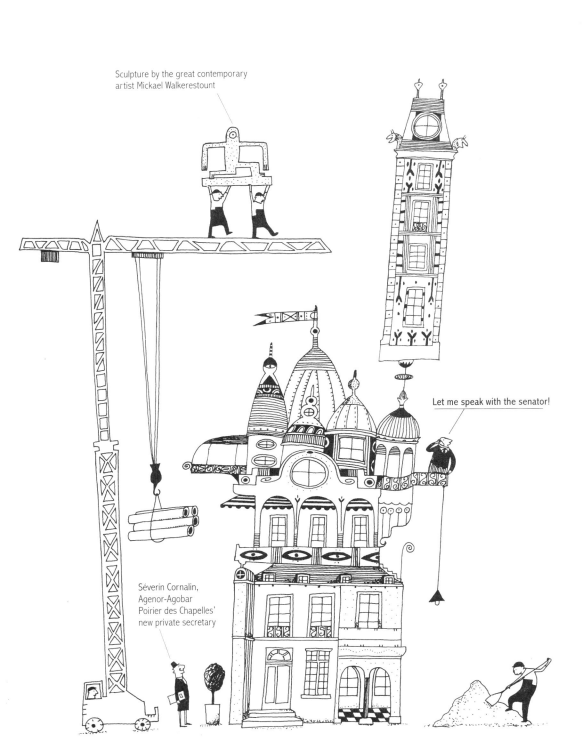

Sculpture by the great contemporary
artist Mickael Walkerestount

Let me speak with the senator!

Séverin Cornalin,
Agenor-Agobar
Poirier des Chapelles'
new private secretary

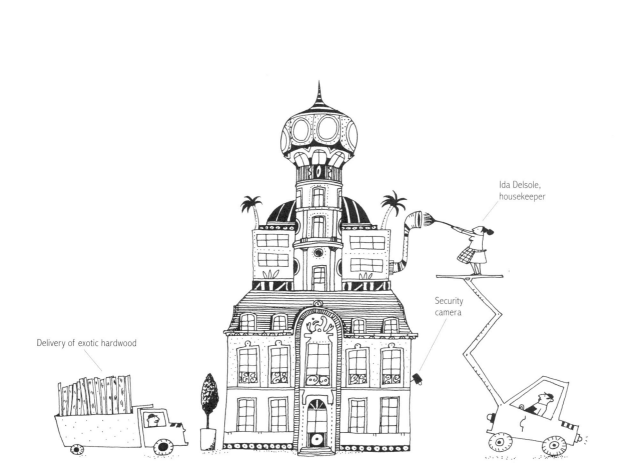

Delivery of exotic hardwood

Ida Delsole,
housekeeper

Security
camera

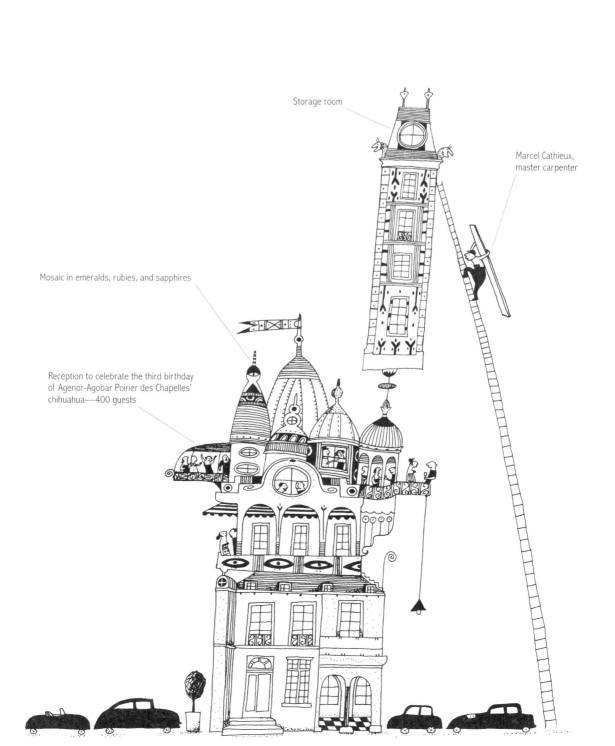

Storage room

Marcel Cathieux,
master carpenter

Mosaic in emeralds, rubies, and sapphires

Reception to celebrate the third birthday
of Agenor-Agobar Poirier des Chapelles'
chihuahua—400 guests

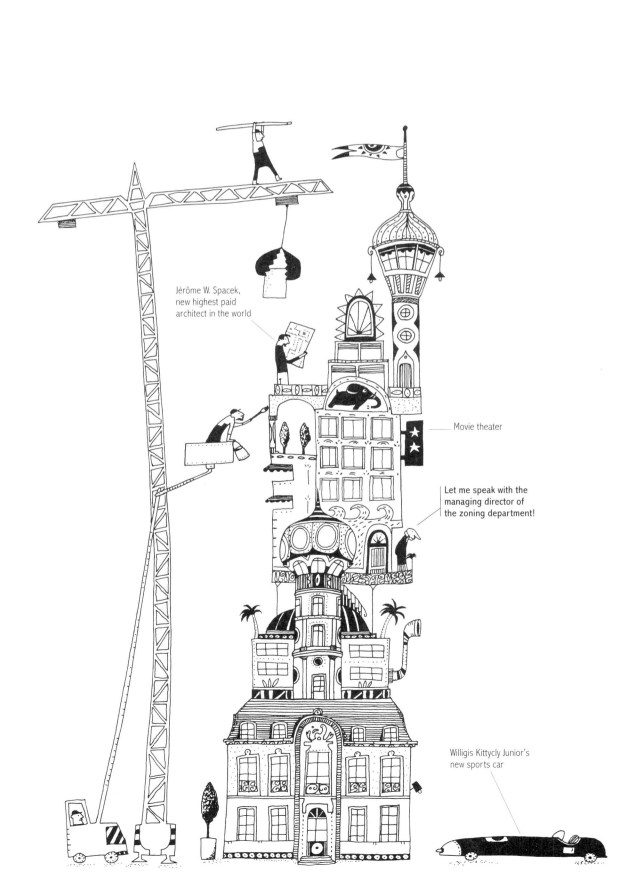

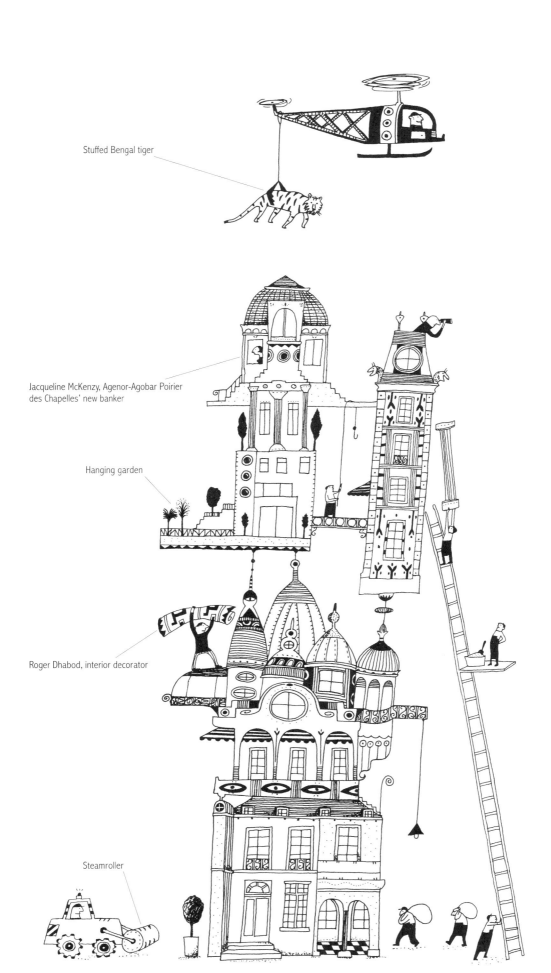

Stuffed Bengal tiger

Jacqueline McKenzy, Agenor-Agobar Poirier
des Chapelles' new banker

Hanging garden

Roger Dhabod, interior decorator

Steamroller

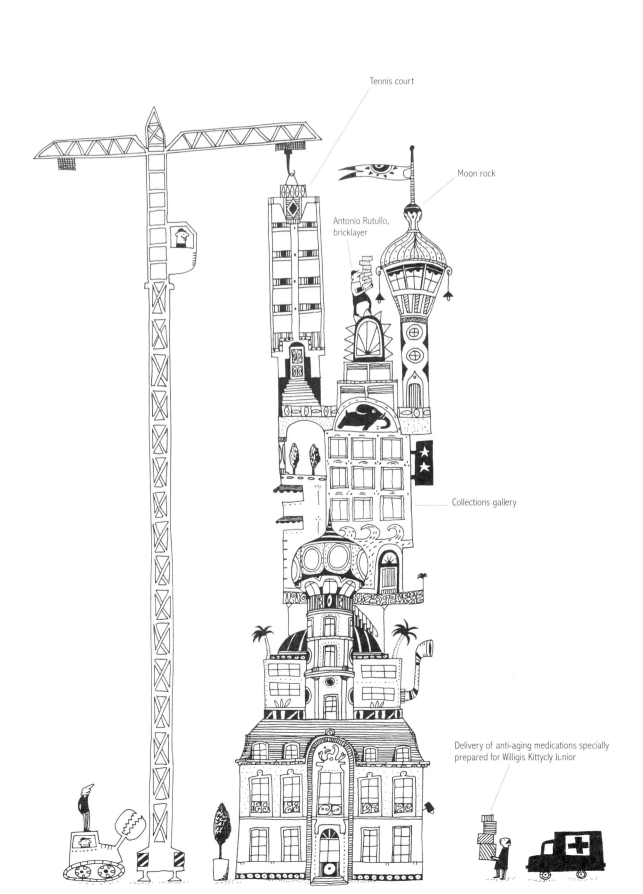

Tennis court

Moon rock

Antonio Rutullo, bricklayer

Collections gallery

Delivery of anti-aging medications specially prepared for Willigis Kittycly Junior

Géraldine Friydeman, new highest paid architect in the world

Parabolic antenna that pulls in all the television stations in the world

Telescopic crane

Let me speak with the Minister of External Affairs!

Furniture by the famous designer Charles Botteka

Agenor-Agobar Poirier des Chapelles' new luxury yacht

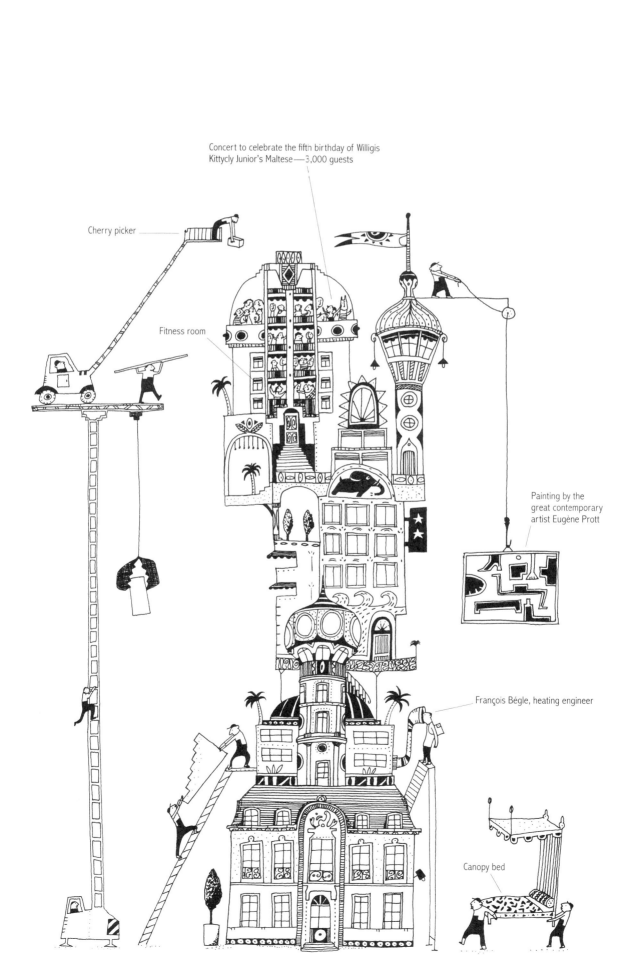

Concert to celebrate the fifth birthday of Willigis
Kittycly Junior's Maltese—3,000 guests

Cherry picker

Fitness room

Painting by the
great contemporary
artist Eugène Prott

François Bégle, heating engineer

Canopy bed

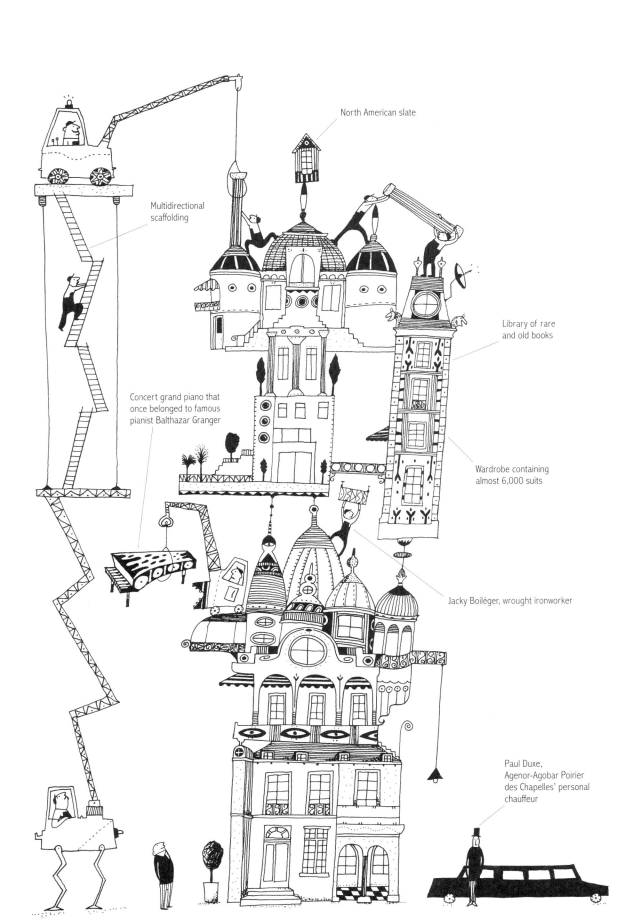

North American slate

Multidirectional
scaffolding

Library of rare
and old books

Concert grand piano that
once belonged to famous
pianist Balthazar Granger

Wardrobe containing
almost 6,000 suits

Jacky Boiléger, wrought ironworker

Paul Duxe,
Agenor-Agobar Poirier
des Chapelles' personal
chauffeur

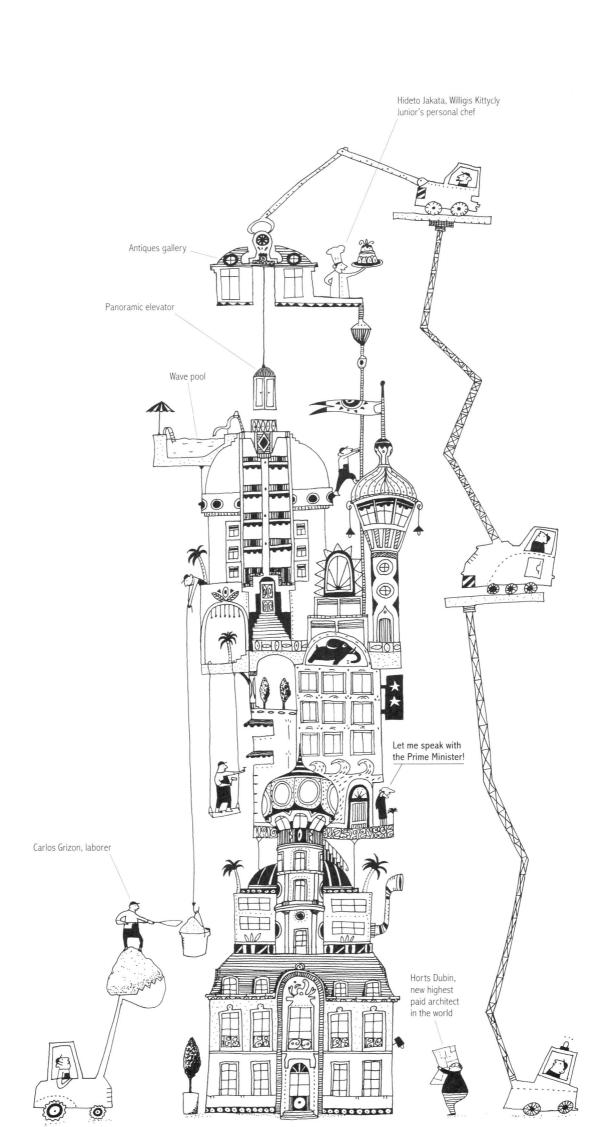

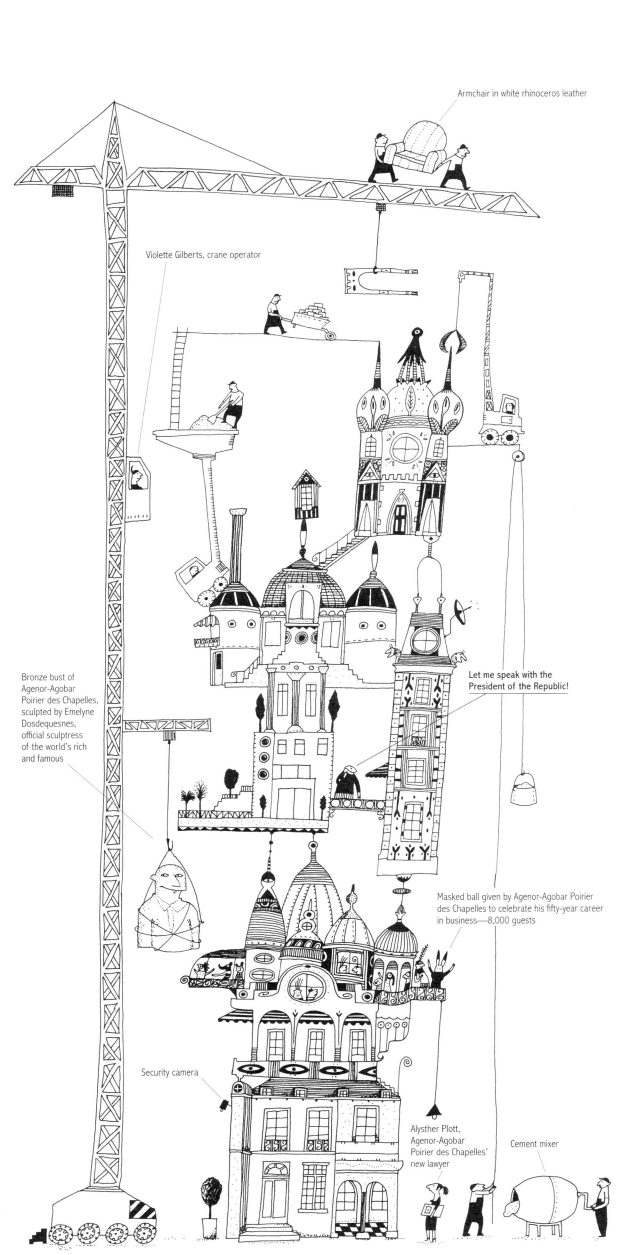

Armchair in white rhinoceros leather

Violette Gilberts, crane operator

Let me speak with the President of the Republic!

Bronze bust of Agenor-Agobar Poirier des Chapelles, sculpted by Emelyne Dosdequesnes, official sculptress of the world's rich and famous

Masked ball given by Agenor-Agobar Poirier des Chapelles to celebrate his fifty-year career in business—8,000 guests

Security camera

Alysther Plott, Agenor-Agobar Poirier des Chapelles' new lawyer

Cement mixer

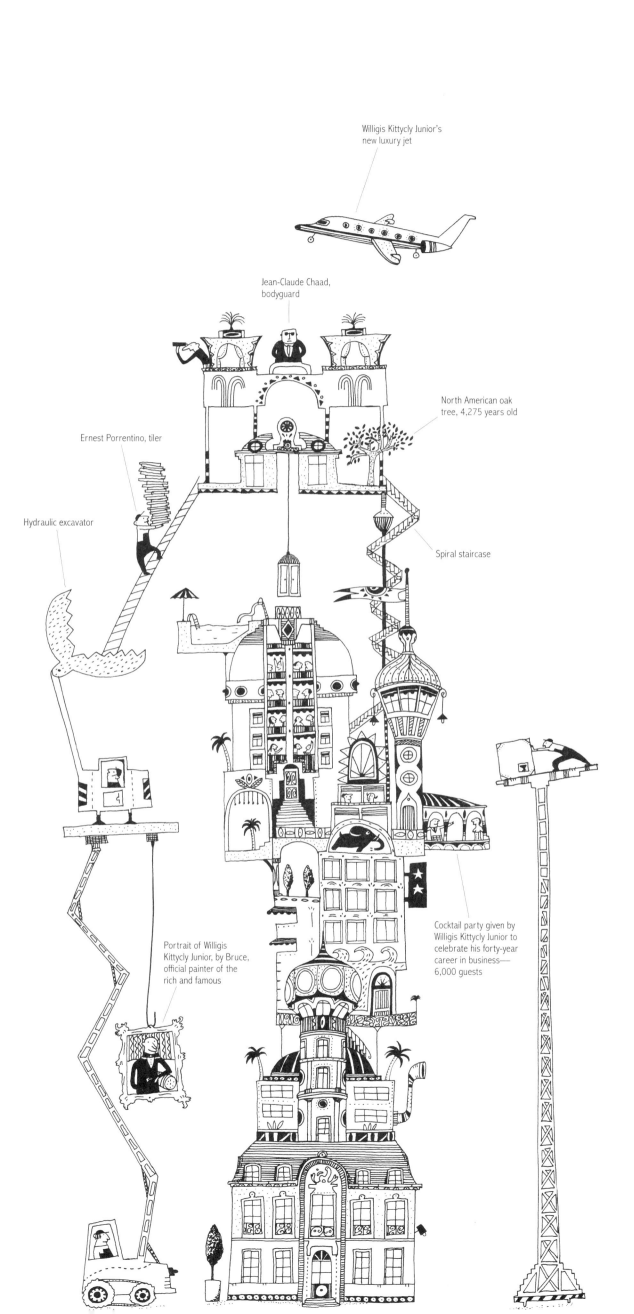

Willigis Kittycly Junior's new luxury jet

Jean-Claude Chaad, bodyguard

North American oak tree, 4,275 years old

Ernest Porrentino, tiler

Hydraulic excavator

Spiral staircase

Portrait of Willigis Kittycly Junior, by Bruce, official painter of the rich and famous

Cocktail party given by Willigis Kittycly Junior to celebrate his forty-year career in business—6,000 guests

It is completely impossible to build any higher,
Mr. Agenor-Agobar Poirier des Chapelles.

Observatory

Yellow parlor

Cabinet
of curiosities

Sam Rochouarde,
carpenter

Murano glass chandelier

Cement truck

Abigail Potell,
Agenor-Agobar
Poirier des Chapelles'
personal hairdresser

Ebony bathtub

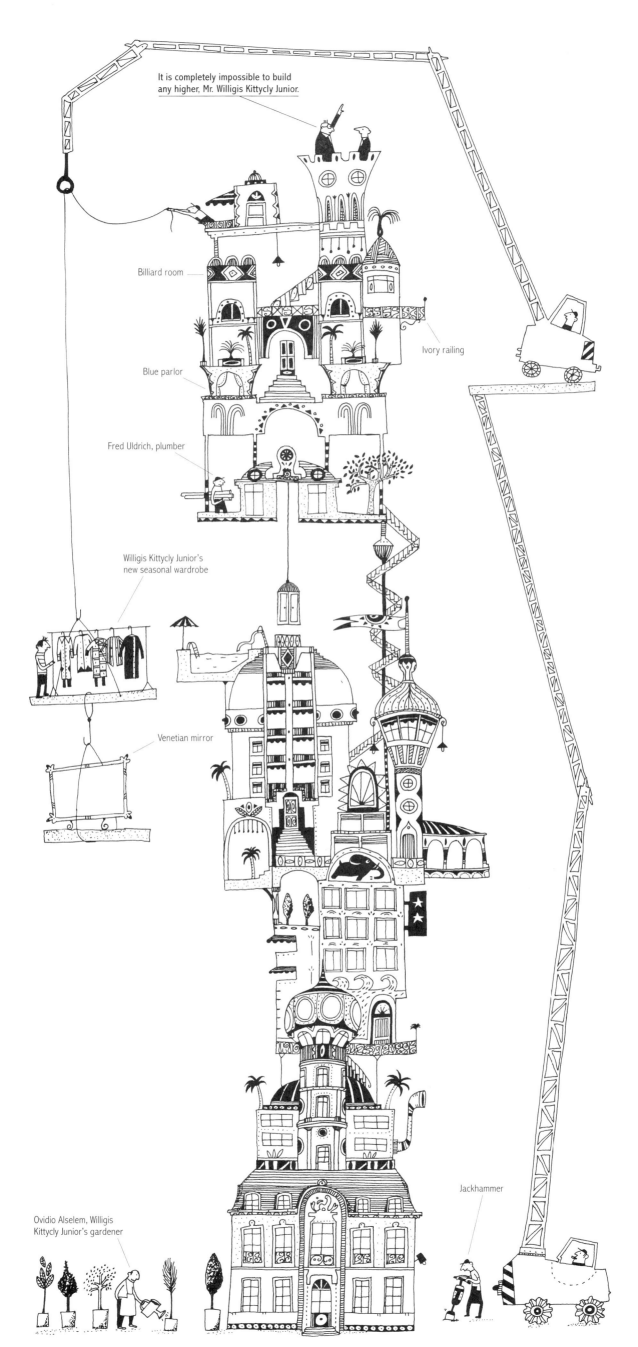

It is completely impossible to build any higher, Mr. Willigis Kittycly Junior.

Billiard room

Blue parlor

Ivory railing

Fred Uldrich, plumber

Willigis Kittycly Junior's new seasonal wardrobe

Venetian mirror

Jackhammer

Ovidio Alselem, Willigis Kittycly Junior's gardener

4,025 feet

Enter the code Q220K785, go up the stairs to the left, go to the end of the hallway, take the elevator to the twentieth floor, take the second door on the left by entering the code WZ347, go up the stairs, turn right and take the elevator to the thirty-sixth floor, walk right to the end of the hallway, go all the way across the central hall, go down the small red staircase, take the elevator in the middle, go up to the sixty-first floor, turn right, go up the spiral staircase, take the elevator on the left, go up to the hundred and sixty-seventh floor, at the end of the hallway, go to the seventh door on the right, enter the code T12H749 and put the pizza on the oval table in the middle of the room!

I'm putting the pizza on the doorstep.
It's easier.

PIZZA

Ludmila Martinot, student

PIZZA